SECURITY DIRECTORATE DOSSIERS

VOLUME 1

Also by Alexandria Blaelock

SHORT STORY COLLECTIONS
The Histories of Hayward Hall
Lovelorn, Lovestruck and Love at First Sight
Common or Garden Variety Heroes
Case Files of the Wilkinson Detective Agency
Unavoidable Fates
Christmas Travesties
Five Faces of Felicia Clarke
Little Place Called Home

FICTION
That Love Nonsense
Taipan vs Brown
The Ghost and Ms Cox
Friends Like That

MS BLAELOCK'S BOOKS
Stress Free Dinner Parties
Signature Wardrobe Planning
Holistic Personal Finance
Minimally Viable Housekeeping
Planning a Life Worth Living

SELECTED SHORT STORIES

Alma's Grace
Balancing the Book
Best Friends Forever
Christmas Bonanza
Christmas Conflagration
Christmas Kisses
Fate in Your Hands
Long Weekend in the Snow
Love in the Past Tense
Mystery of the Master Suite
Needy Bitch
Remains of Christmas
Secret Singer
Shining Star
Ship in a Bottle

Simone Says Hands in the Air
Special Relativity in Space
The Bygone Boyfriend
The Day the Schedule Broke
The Ghost Detectors
The Kiss of Death
The Mince Pie Mystery
The Palace Hotel
The Pseudonym's Bride
The Shadow Thieves
The Space Time Paradox
Toy Soldiers
Waylon's Way

SECURITY DIRECTORATE DOSSIERS

VOLUME 1

ALEXANDRIA BLAELOCK

BlueMere Books
MELBOURNE, AUSTRALIA

For permission requests, please contact enquiries@bluemerebooks.com.

Ordering Information:
Discounts are available on quantity purchases. For details, contact orders@bluemerebooks.com.

Security Directorate Dossiers volume 1/Alexandria Blaelock
hardback ISBN: 978-1-922744-70-8
paperback ISBN: 978-1-922744-71-5
digital ISBN: 978-1-922744-72-2
AI generated audio: 978-1-922744-73-9

Book Layout © BookDesignTemplates.com
Cover Art © Tithi Luadthong/depositphotos

Contents

INTRODUCTION

One thing writers have in common with children is the ability to construct whole new worlds with about five minutes of daydreaming,

Children imagine being a firefighter one day, and a ballet dancer the next. Life with different parents, and with more, or less, siblings.

One day they colour everything yellow, and the next blue. They might pull up a baby carrot and consider carrots that might grow as far as the other side of the planet.

Writers do the same, and our imaginations can be just as wild. Worlds governed by magic instead of physics? Worlds ruled by women? Ruled by lizards? No problems whatsoever.

I find I'm inspired by the books I read, and the tv shows I watch. Sometimes I might think it's stupid and rewrite it, others I'll use it as a launching pad.

The Security Directorate comes from a strange combination of old and new wars.

Starting with a bunch of documentaries about the Third Reich. How they came to power, how they ruled, how the ruling elite were so much better off than the ordinary people. Not to mention the assassination attempts on the leader.

And ghoulishly fascinating, the policies of eugenics with involuntary sterilisation, genocide and experimentation with breeding programs.

Meanwhile, the Syrian Civil War had reached its peak. It continues with an uneasy peace and sporadic outbreaks of tension and violence.

This "peace" is unchanged either by the condemnation of international leaders or, more recently, earthquakes.

Which got me thinking. What if something like the Third Reich erupted today?

The rest of the planet is reluctant to intervene in conflicts, even where it is possible to do so.

And more recently, we've seen a solid programme of propaganda and indoctrination could work.

So, what would life be like in today's fascist dictatorship? One that included an Office of Public Enlightenment and a Genomics Bureau?

Where you were bred and indoctrinated to blindly follow orders.

These speculative stories attempt to explain how it might work. To take you through the potential stages of your life:

- In *Life in the Security Directorate*, Eve struggles to come to terms with life in the Directorate, and finds her own way out.

- While *Love in the Security Directorate* shows us while they might control who you marry, they can't always control who you fall in love with.

- Lieutenant Jemima Hunt discovers in *Success at the Academy*, the power over life or death is not always clear cut.

• Moving on, in *Payton's Run*, one student makes it through the live fire physical assessment.

• And finally, in *Minty and the Monster*, we join Second Lieutenant Minty Hollister at her first post.

In the unlikely event a Security Directorate set itself up in Australia, I expect I'd find myself at death's door in a desert re-education camp. Would that be lucky for me? I can't say for sure.

Alexandria Blaelock
Melbourne, Australia
April, 2023

ALEXANDRIA BLAELOCK

AUTHOR OF FATE IN YOUR HANDS

LIFE IN THE SECURITY DIRECTORATE

A SECURITY DIRECTORATE SHORT STORY

LIFE IN THE SECURITY DIRECTORATE

Eve closed her eyes and leaned her forehead against the stationery cupboard door. Most of her days were pretty shitty, but for some reason, this one was shittier than most.

Maybe not the shittiest day of her life, that was probably the day she'd been born.

After she passed the Genomics Bureau postnatal testing, her parents had quickly signed her and all her rights over to the State. She was remanded to the State Academy of Cultural Regulation while her parents tried to live down the shame of producing what was colloquially known as a superhero.

She took a deep calming breath.

What was it she needed right now?

Black Earl Grey tea with a thin slice of lemon. And a lemon shortbread biscuit to go with it. In a nice vintage, rose-patterned bone china cup and saucer.

She pulled the cupboard door open, and there it was, steaming gently on top of a stack of notebooks.

She smoothed a few stray mouse-brown loose hairs back into her long ponytail and took her tea back to her desk.

Kicking off her sensible shoes, she pulled open the bottom drawer of her broken pedestal unit, pulled out a small cushion which she placed on her desk and propped her feet up on it.

Drawing the silence around her like a cloak of invisibility, she closed her eyes and inhaled the tea's citrus aroma before taking a sip.

Designated FX-84325, she'd been given all the love and care you'd expect of a State-run Academy - bullying, intensive education, hard physical work, mind control and so on.

Instead of being trained to fit in, the children were intensively trained to stand out. At least they were if they didn't die during basic training.

Survivors had no choice but to join the Protection Squadron. The terrifyingly impassive guardians of whatever the State named the public good.

No friends or family to influence their rigid, unbiased and unthinking law enforcement.

During the fiercely competitive initial training, she hadn't displayed a useful skill, like reading or influencing minds, blowing up or moving heavy loads or getting places really fast.

Subsequently, she'd been redesignated FG-84325, and shunted into general training for low-level operatives; colloquially known as goons.

She rotated her shoulders a few times and rocked her head back and forth across them to try and relieve the tension and stiffness.

As bad as her subsequent life had been, Eve was grateful she'd been declared faulty and expelled from the programme.

As a failed superhero, she at least had the chance of a somewhat normal life.

It wasn't easy though - the Directorate sent out undercover agents as failed superheroes too, so you were greeted with suspicion wherever you went. It was very rare anyone would trust or want to get to know you.

Now designated Eve, the State mandated name for failed female operatives, with a permanent record of attendance at superhero school, the population treated her as warily as a jaguar zoo escapee.

Not to mention that expulsion left her standing outside the school gates with just the clothes on her back.

No family, no money, no support. Presumably, given the training, the idea was to ensure you didn't survive on your own.

She dunked her biscuit in the tea and savoured the flavour as it slowly dissolved on her tongue.

Eve had always been lucky. She'd always been able to lay her hands on whatever she needed. Whether that was an extra food ration, a safe place to hide, or a helping hand. Or maybe that was her superpower.

Undetected, because she needed it to be.

For her, it was a pretty useful power to have, even though it wasn't always reliable. She wasn't sure how need was determined, or what would meet that need.

Or where the stuff came from. Or given it disappeared when she was done needing it, what happened to it.

She took a deep breath and stretched as she let it out in a sigh.

Her ability to quickly obtain required supplies with a minimum of fuss had earned her a tiny, yet private office in the warehouse.

It was gloomy, full of broken furniture and a long way from where the business action happened.

But it was all hers.

Plus, her unwavering cheerfulness in the face of constant doubt had gained her a certain amount of tolerance from her colleagues.

She would always be an outsider, but she was treated reasonably well and accepted at company functions.

Though, fearing alcohol-fuelled reprisals for Protection Squad activities, she always managed to leave before the drinking started in earnest.

She didn't know for sure, but it made sense the Squad would monitor her activities more carefully than normals, so she'd been vigilant.

In general, she lived a quiet life, skirting the fringes of other people's lives. She kept to herself, dressed and acted to avoid attention, and tried not to use her power unless it was necessary.

But she was lonely. She worked alone, then went home alone, to her tiny apartment full of smiling stuffed animals. She bought cookbooks from exotic places she would never be permitted to visit and cooked single-serve meals.

After dinner, she curled up in a blanket, reading borrowed books, living an adventurous kind of life with close friends forbidden to her.

Imagining she was allowed a boyfriend, someone to kiss and openly share her feelings with.

Today's borrowed tea and biscuit was relatively minor - a quiet moment outside of normal. Once she'd been followed into a building, and exited from another in someone else's body.

She sighed again, put the empty teacup down, and massaged her temples. Just for a moment, she imagined another life.

One where the State didn't monitor and control the people. Where there was no such thing as a Protection Squad, and people lived their lives freely and openly.

What would that be like?

Standing up, she stretched again and walked across the room to the window overlooking the warehouse. The sun was shining, birds were singing, and a warm, soft floral breeze blew through a crack in the glass.

Given the opportunity, she'd have climbed out the window to see what that other life was like, but the bars made that impossible.

For the moment she'd satisfy herself with a borrowed breath of fresh air.

The stiff office door scraped and jittered as someone tried to open it.

Eve turned away from the window and walked towards her desk. By the time she got there, the room had reverted to its usual dingy appearance.

The sunny exterior view faded to a dirty safety glass window overlooking the warehouse. The cushion, teacup and saucer also disappeared.

An odour of must rolled over the light scent of flowers.

She stepped back into her shoes, smoothed her grey pencil skirt down and kicked the pedestal drawer shut.

Then picked up a notebook covered in a girly cartoon pattern from her neat and clean desk, along with a pencil topped by a half-used rabbit eraser.

She pasted a cheerful smile on her face and was ready to take on whoever came through the door.

It suddenly gave way, and a tall, well-dressed muscular man fell through, tripping a few steps forward to collide with her.

She deftly caught and held him to stop him falling over. Trying not to inhale his brisk outdoorsy scent, she let him catch his balance.

He quickly took a step back. While it was probably for his own protection, Eve was grateful to have more air around her.

"I'm sorry, the door's sticky. I've called the maintenance department, but it's a very low priority."

He smiled and waved a hand in its direction, "there's no need. It's not your fault."

Eve smiled a small smile and bowed her head in acknowledgement.

"I'm Adam, I'm here about the Statutory Department's order for half a pallet of copy paper."

Eve looked a little more closely at him. His name labelled him a failed superhero just like her, but his clothing suggested he was an agent.

She'd never met another failure and didn't know what to expect.

She schooled her face, trying not to look too alarmed or interested. She was fairly sure she hadn't done anything to raise suspicion, but he could still be there for a random audit.

She put her notebook and pencil down and nodded professionally. "I've prepared your order for dispatch. If you'll follow me, I'll show you where it is."

She opened the warehouse door and led him down the steel stairs, his eyes boring holes in her back.

Not literally, of course, he was a failure too, but her recently relaxed shoulders started tensing up again anyway.

As they walked through the racked stock, Eve was at war with herself.

On one side, she was eaten up with curiosity about who he was and how he came to be there.

Even though she was essentially quarantined from the normals, she thought someone might have mentioned there was another failure in the building.

Or were there so many of them by now that it barely rated a mention?

On the other side, who was he, and why was he there? Was he auditing her?

Was he involved in some other State ordered action, even if he was only the copy boy? Did he know she was an Eve?

How did he fail out of the Academy?

But as they moved further away from her office, the silence lengthened. All too soon they'd reached the stacked trolley, and it was too late to ask anything at all.

Eve put her cheerful face back on and nodded her ponytailed head at the trolley, "here we are - all stacked up and ready to go. Can you manage from here?"

He gave the trolley an experimental push and smiled ruefully. "I think I'll be okay with the trolley, but I'm new here and have no idea how to get back to my workstation."

Eve nodded once, "are you on the Statutory Department floor?"

"I guess so."

"Fine, I can take you back," she gestured toward the side of the warehouse, "this way."

He took the trolley, made a small u-turn to get it going, and headed in the direction she'd pointed.

Determined not to lose this second opportunity, she stepped up and walked beside him, "have you been with us long?"

"About a week. I'm here collating some documents to send to the Office of Public Enlightenment."

"I see, do you work for Public Enlightenment?"

Adam snorted, "do you really think with the name Adam I'd be working for Public Enlightenment? I'm just an admin temp; here to fetch coffee, sharpen pencils and do the copying."

Eve pursed her lips for a moment. He seemed very open about his failure, but other than that, it was too soon to trust him, "I understand."

"I heard there's an Eve here somewhere, do you know where I might find her?"

Eve gasped and stepped back, what did he want with an Eve?

And did he want an Eve, or did he want her?

Adam turned to look quizzically at her suddenly shuttered face.

"I am Eve, what do you want with me."

He held out in supplication, "I'm sorry, I didn't mean to scare you. I just overheard a conversation about you and wanted to meet you. I've never met another failure before."

His answer was a little too much like what she wanted to hear.

If she was an agent, it'd be the kind of thing she'd say to try and gain trust. But at the same time, it was exactly what she'd been thinking about him.

Was this her superpower trying to give her what she needed?

She frowned at him, "then you'll know that just makes you seem more like an agent than a failure. What did you overhear?"

"Essentially, that you seem so nice and normal, they can't believe you're a superhero. They were speculating that something went wrong during your postnatal testing and you'd been misdiagnosed. I've never heard anything like it before."

Eve slumped back against the racking. If, in fact, any of that was true, it was high praise from her colleagues. But could he or they really be trusted?

Her empty heart really hoped so.

She needed a chocolate, and wondering vaguely what he might need, reached hopefully into the stock behind her. She pulled out a packet and without looking at it, opened it and offered him first go.

"Oh my god, it's salted macadamias, my favourite! Where did you get them?"

That answered the question about whether she could pick up what other people needed. "I spend most of my time down here, and it's too tiresome to keep running up the stairs to the office, so I stash snacks about the place. Would you like something to drink?"

Adam smiled, "how about a delicious can of State Regulated Cola then?"

To give her story some substance, she handed over the nuts, darted out of sight round around the rack and came back with two lukewarm cans.

He laughed, clenched the nut packet between his teeth and reached for a can.

He opened it and handed it back before taking the other. "I guess your colleagues are right, you *are* too normal to be a superhero."

Eve blushed prettily and put on her cheerful face, "you're too kind. What about you, were you misdiagnosed as well?"

Going by the shock in his face, it was probably a little too intimate too soon. She took a quick gulp of the drink and came up choking.

He pounded her back to help clear her airways.

Once her coughs had subsided, she said "I'm sorry Adam, that was very presumptuous of me. Please forget I asked."

"No, it's not that," he said, sipping his drink, "it's just that like you, I'm not used to people talking to me."

He hooked a big box from the bottom rack with his foot and gestured for her to sit before snagging one for himself.

"Partway through the skills assessment, I became ill and lost my ability. The Academy tried a variety of treatments, but couldn't bring it back."

He shrugged, "after a couple of years of experimentation, I was invalided out."

It was a plausible story, but it had taken her decades of hard work to make the pitiful career progress she'd made.

How did he come to be wearing a high-quality suit working with classified information for the Office of Public Enlightenment?

She took a more careful drink. "So you work for the Security Directorate now?"

He looked at her in disbelief, "I'm sorry, I don't get how you came to that conclusion?"

Eve gestured at his suit pants, "well, you're an overly confident, fit and healthy failed superhero wearing a decent suit. Why would anyone think you were anything other than an agent?"

He snorted, "I can see why you'd think that, but I'm Adam Rochester of the Signals Department Rochesters. They didn't renounce me when I was invalided out of the Academy. Came close though."

Well, that made all the difference - rich boy from a cultural elite family with all the benefits that brought him.

"So you just get preferential treatment because your family's high up in the political hierarchy?"

"Well not entirely, the law is still the law, regardless of who your family is. I'm still Adam - I can't be a superhero, and I can't live a normal life."

He closed his eyes for a moment and took a swig from the can. "My family tolerates me, but I'm still a failure in their eyes. It just means they're compelled to take care of me, though they've made it plain they expect me to take care of myself and not drain their resources."

He smiled evilly, "I bet they regret setting up a trust fund for me as well as not renouncing me."

Eve drained her drink and left the empty can on the rack. Dare she conduct an experiment of her own?

Failed superheroes aren't permitted physical contact, but she needed to know whether he was friend or foe, so she daringly nudged his shoulder with her own.

"I sometimes wonder what it would be like to live somewhere else where these rules don't apply don't you?"

He frowned a little, but made no mention of the contact, "I can't imagine living anywhere else, but maybe more like a normal. To have friends and parties - to be welcomed, not shunned."

They sat in companionable silence, each trying to imagine a future that wasn't State controlled.

He sighed, "I've been gone a while, I suppose I should get back to my copying."

Eve echoed his sigh, she didn't think it had been that long of a break, and agent or not, she really didn't want to let him go, "it's been nice, thanks for taking the time to chat."

She stood and placed his empty nut bag and can with her own "the goods lift is this way."

He stood, dusted his hands on his pants and kicked the boxes back into their places in the rack, "do you want me to take the rubbish?"

"No thanks, I'll get rid of it when I get back."

He gave the trolley a solid push to get it moving again, and they crossed the final space to the lift.

Eve pushed the up button, "if the lift opened to a parallel universe, would you get in?"

He glanced at her, "Now who sounds like an agent?"

She laughed, "I know, but what's the worst that can happen? We get euthanised?"

"Don't you think they'd torture you for information or something before they kill you?"

"I don't know, it's not something you hear about, is it? Not knowing, and imagining is worse than knowing for sure."

The lift binged, "last chance" she shouted, "in or out?"

He opened his mouth, she wasn't sure whether it was to scream or answer her question, but the lift doors opened to reveal the padded walls of the goods lift, and it was too late.

She waited for him to manoeuvre the trolley into the carriage before entering herself and pushing the button for the 57th floor. She stood to the side, facing Adam, hands clasped in front of her.

He flinched as it shuddered and dropped slightly before starting its ascent. "Why would you even think about parallel universes?" he asked.

"I think it's the nature of all humans, superhero or normal, to seek freedom and happiness. What about you and your friends and parties? Aren't you tired of living alone?"

"I suppose. But, given I'm a Rochester, I'm never really alone. Though I get all the Rochester obligations without the benefits. It would be nice to please myself occasionally."

"Can I take that as Yes! I'll get off at the closest parallel universe?"

He jiggled the trolley as he thought, "You know what, I might be wrong, but I can't see how it could be worse than here. Aside from arriving there with nothing."

"Like the ultimate refugee - nothing to lose and everything to gain."

He laughed awkwardly, "yes, I suppose so."

The lift binged as they approached their destination, and Adam bunched his muscles, preparing to push the trolley out into the corridor.

The doors opened to reveal a lush green meadow, drenched in sunshine. Eve pushed the button that held the doors open.

The wind bent the grass, pushing the fresh scent of the open countryside into the carriage. A butterfly flew in, found no flowers and flew out again.

Adam's jaw dropped, and he rubbed his eyes as if he couldn't believe what he was seeing.

She smiled at him, "we've reached our destination. Do you want to please yourself enough to follow me?"

His once-friendly face contorted, and he snarled, "I knew you were too good to be true."

It seemed he was an undercover agent after all. He tried to get out from behind the trolley, but right now, she needed him to stay where he was, and the trolley wheels obliged.

He lunged at her as she stepped out onto the grass, but he just succeeded in dislodging boxes of paper and fencing himself in.

Perhaps he was just afraid, "this really is your last chance Adam, once the doors close, they'll reopen, and you'll be back at the Statutory Department. Neither one thing nor the other."

"I don't know what you've done to me, but there is no other universe. I'm placing you under arrest - get back in this lift."

The wind pulled her hair loose from her ponytail, and it crackled around her head like electricity.

"You know I can't do that Adam. My sad life was over the minute you entered my building. I don't know where I am, or if my power will work here. But no matter what, I'm better off here."

He snarled and lunged again.

"This really is your last chance Adam. We don't even have to stay together. You can make your own path to your future."

"There is nothing for me there that I don't have here. For all I know, it will be worse there. You'll probably be eaten by lions."

She smiled sadly, "thanks for showing me what I missed Adam. I wish you a future of freedom and happiness."

Eve didn't need an escape route, so she raised a hand in farewell, let the lift doors close with a final clunk and disappear.

She stretched and took a deep breath of fresh air. It didn't matter where she went, so she closed her eyes and spun around a few times, then started walking. She couldn't wait to see what this world had to offer.

THE END

ALEXANDRIA
BLAELOCK
AUTHOR OF FATE IN YOUR HANDS
LOVE IN THE
SECURITY
DIRECTORATE
A SECURITY DIRECTORATE SHORT STORY

LOVE IN THE SECURITY DIRECTORATE

Captain Seraphina Robinson forced herself to take a power stance; spine straight, feet slightly spread, hands lightly clasped behind her back as she coolly observed her "husband" to be.

She knew of Major Callan Muir of course, they'd met at the University of Civilisation.

Technically the University was open to all citizens.

But everyone knew it was only for those who survived the State Academy of Cultural Regulation and were destined for high positions within the Protection Squadron.

And to get into the Academy, you needed a Genomics Bureau classification proving you had a certain kind of genetic ability. The kind known colloquially as a "superpower."

Ideally achieved through the Directorate eugenics programme.

She'd admired his quiet stillness and was fascinated by his deep, resonant and commanding voice. Perhaps that was his "superpower", though you never spoke of those.

He was very popular, always the centre of a group of sycophantic women.

Rumour had it he'd ended more than one promising career with unsanctioned intimate relationships.

She knew her career would end soon enough, but she'd wanted to make the best of it while she could.

He was only an inch or two taller than her, yet he and his fresh citrus cologne seemed to take up too much space in the tiny office they stood in.

His sleek dark hair, precisely cut to Regulation length and style, was slightly crimped by the peaked cap now lightly gripped between his body and arm.

He was fortunate; his head and body shape were ideally suited to his black officer's dress uniform.

And that his medals took up an impressive amount of space across his broad chest.

She enjoyed a quiet moment of gratitude that her husband was attractive.

And around her age.

Unlike poor Asrani, who was paired with a fat ugly man twice her age. Though they seemed to get on well enough.

And according to Asrani, he was faithful to her too.

It was too soon to tell what kind of husband the Major would be.

History suggested not faithful, but you didn't gain rapid advancement by taking stupid risks.

Maybe it was just a matter of the time you needed to get to know your partner.

She took a deep breath and resisted the urge to touch the smooth, clear skin of his face.

She scratched the palm of her hand instead.

He didn't seem to have aged a day.

Major Muir turned smartly as the Registrar pushed the door open, and entered with a large, red leather-bound ledger.

He sat at the desk and opened the book.

"The Genomics Bureau has paired you, Major Callan Muir, with you Captain Seraphina Robinson, in an exclusive and binding five-year contract.

"You will now live together until the Bureau sees fit to terminate the contract between you.

"Do you declare before me, that you come here voluntarily, and are without reservation prepared to do as the Bureau requires?"

"I do," they replied simultaneously.

"Major Muir," the Registrar said, "repeat after me; I Major Callan Muir, take Captain Seraphina Robinson as my allocated spouse to love, respect and care for."

Without hesitation, he did. And then it was her turn.

"I, Captain Seraphina Robinson, take Major Callan Muir as my allocated spouse to love, respect, and care for."

"Well done," the Registrar said, "I know you didn't have much notice, but were you able to get rings?"

Callan pulled a fancifully engraved silver coloured band from his pocket.

"Major Muir, please place your ring on Captain Robinson's finger as a symbol of your commitment to her, and submission to the will of the State."

His hands were comfortingly warm against her cold ones. Firm and soft as he took her left hand and placed the ring, warm from his pocket, on her finger.

"Captain Robinson?" the Registrar asked.

She fidgeted, "I was notified of the union and recalled from my mission this morning. I don't have a ring."

"Not to worry," said the Registrar pulling open a drawer in the desk, "you may use this band until you get an appropriate replacement.

"Captain Robinson, please place the ring on Major Muir's finger as a symbol of your commitment to him, and submission to the will of the State."

She took the cold and heavy ring from the Registrar and, slipped it on Callan's finger.

"Excellent." The Registrar offered Callan a pen, "if you'd sign the register please."

Callan signed with a neat, compact signature and handed the pen to her. She signed her name and gave the pen back to the Registrar.

"Congratulations on your union. You may kiss."

They exchanged the required cheek kisses, right, left, right, and that was it.

They were "married," as the normals called it. At least for the time being.

"Your belongings are being transferred to your new quarters," he scribbled on a paper and passed it to Callan.

"Here's the address. May your union be long and fruitful."

They inclined their heads respectfully to the Registrar. Callan replaced his cap, turned to her and offered his ring-clad hand.

She pursed her lips slightly but took it.

As they left the room, she took a deep breath of unscented air, though it didn't dissipate the strength of his presence of the heat of his hand.

They walked down the corridor to the lift well, where she pushed the down button.

Now she was partnered with someone she barely knew.

The match probably had very little to do with them, and more to do with the offspring they might produce.

While she was mildly curious about what they hoped the children would be, it didn't really matter.

If they passed the Genomics Bureau's post-natal testing, they'd be sent to the Academy as she'd been, and it was unlikely she'd see them again.

And if they didn't, well, it was unlikely she'd see them again.

She glanced up at Callan, to see his full lips smiling slightly, and quickly looked away. Her heart skipped a beat, and she swallowed nervously.

What did you say to someone you barely knew but had entered a State-sanctioned relationship with?

It wasn't as if the children couldn't be made in the lab, so it was more likely they were supposed to monitor each other.

After all their training, was it even possible they'd be able to trust each other enough to love, respect, and care for each other?

Hopefully.

Seraphina wanted someone to love, respect, and care for her, but did he?

More importantly, *would* he?

Mind you, if there were no children, it probably wouldn't be a long union so it wouldn't matter anyway.

He gave her hand a light squeeze, "it's an odd situation isn't it?"

Her smile was more of a grimace as she turned to look at him again.

Partnered or not, it was unseemly to touch in public, so she pulled her hand, but he didn't release it.

"I didn't expect to be paired so soon after graduation."

"It's not really that soon, it's been five years."

"I know, but I didn't imagine I'd be called back mid-assignment for this."

She sighed, "I've important work to complete, and it'll be months before I'm permitted to return."

"I agree marriage doesn't seem as important as some other matters, Captain Robinson, but perhaps you'll find it easier if you think of it as a new assignment with different objectives."

She looked at him sharply, but he seemed serious.

And, perhaps it was good advice - was that the key to a long and fruitful union?

She licked her lips.

At some point, the fruitful part had to be a factor.

The lift arrived, and the occupants looked curiously at them as they shuffled around to make room. It wasn't often you saw people touching in public, let alone with bare skin. Callan entered, pulling her in behind him.

《《 • 》》

Callan was so happy.

He'd known from the moment he first saw her at University, that she was the one he wanted to spend his life with.

Her fitted uniform emphasised her curves in the best possible way, and the seams of her stockings were as straight as her spine.

Her fiery red hair was smoothed into the regulation chignon, though a lock had fallen loose and curled seductively down her straight back.

Then she'd turned around, and they'd locked eyes for a moment before someone stole her attention away. But it was enough.

She'd glowed, literally glowed, like a bright golden beacon on the edge of the dark group she was with.

He'd tried to get closer as their time at University progressed, but somehow she'd always slipped away at the last minute.

She glowed when she saw him, and he didn't see her glowing at anyone else.

He wanted to know more.

Not that unauthorised relationships were permitted, and she was clearly the kind of person who followed the rules.

So, he formed a plan and learned what he could from the women who'd made themselves available to him.

And how the time had finally come, he was ready for her.

It had taken almost the entire intervening period to prove himself and his precognitive abilities.

He'd progressed quickly up the ranks so that when he said Seraphina was to be allocated to him, no one doubted it was true.

And even though he hadn't in truth seen any such thing, when he saw her glow burst out as he'd entered the Registrar's office, all his doubts were laid to rest.

Even her light floral fragrance had reached out towards him.

He wondered if her power involved light and clarity, but you didn't ever talk about that.

Least of all in enclosed spaces where it was highly likely you were being monitored.

Like their new home probably would be.

Still holding hands, they exited the lift.

She'd stopped trying to free herself the minute he'd pulled her into the lift, and when they reached the coat check, he was reluctant to let her go.

Though now they were paired, there was nowhere else she could go.

He held out her greatcoat so she could easily slip her arms into the sleeves, and lingered perhaps a moment too long as he smoothed it across her shoulders.

She was his to do as he wanted with, but he wanted her to love, respect, and care for him.

As he already did for her.

He shrugged into his own greatcoat, imagining how sweet the future would be in a union of affection, not just duty.

As they left the building, he took her hand and tucked it through his arm before putting his hand in his pocket.

The contours of her body fit neatly against his own, "it's a beautiful day, and it's not far to our new home, shall we walk?"

She shrugged, and her whole body moved against him, a chaste preview of the passion he hoped was to come.

There was no rush, newly partnered officers were granted several week's leave as a matter of course, so he set a leisurely pace.

It seemed the sun lit up the street ahead of them, though he hoped it was her.

"How have you been since University Major Muir?"

"Well that feels a little awkward now we're partnered, doesn't it? Please call me Callan."

She nodded once, "of course Callan. You may call me Sera."

"Thank you, Sera. Obviously, I can't tell you about the classified work I've been doing, but I've been well. How about you?"

"About the same Callan," her cheeks coloured slightly, "I was excited to have the opportunity to travel with my work. Did you?"

"No, I've been based here in the City. Now and again, I get a leave pass and take a day trip to the countryside. Perhaps I can visit you when you return to your post?"

"I expect that would be acceptable."

He winced, but she probably hadn't spent the intervening period obsessively following his career the way he had hers.

Somehow, she'd fallen into step with him, so that was a hopeful sign.

And she'd left her hand where he'd put it, so he risked covering it with his own. "Have you spent much time in the City then?"

"Only periodic visits for planning sessions and further training. I don't think it's changed much since University."

"Here and there." He knew she'd studied Ancient History at University, and thought he could tempt her.

"They opened the New Ancient History Museum last year, we could visit it together if you like?"

She looked up at him, "I'm not sure it would be your thing, but yes, I'd like that."

He smiled down at her and inwardly pumped his fist in the air.

A brave street urchin approached the Protection Squadron officers, "five dollars for a rose for the lady sir?"

The blossom was probably stolen, but he bought a red one anyway and leaning across, held it to her nose to smell.

Its sweet perfume seemed to pull them closer together.

He looked at her lips, and she licked them, then blushed daintily.

He pinned the rose to the collar of her coat, then tucked her hand back into the crook of his arm.

All too soon they were standing on the footpath outside the ugly yet compelling Brutalist-style building housing their new apartment.

The sun slanting through the clouds gave it a golden halo as they looked up at its stark horizontal lines.

Her jaw dropped a little, "it's beautiful, but surely there's some kind of mistake. This is much too lavish."

"Well, I am a Major, and we do have a position to maintain."

It wasn't too far from the truth, but he'd called in a few favours to have one of the smaller apartments allocated to them as a residence.

And they should be able to make some favourable connections from this base. "Let's go in and see what it's like."

He opened the door for her, allowing her to enter first.

But now that it was his home, even he was a little over-awed by the brightly lit, highly polished concrete foyer.

A uniformed concierge with a small sidearm approached, "Major Muir, Captain Robinson?" They nodded in reply.

"This way please, you're in apartment 1202," He escorted them to the lift, and pushed the call button.

"Your things have been unpacked, and the apartment made ready for your arrival."

When the lift arrived, he gestured for them to enter the brass lined capsule before following and pressing the button for the twelfth floor.

《《 • 》》

Sera stepped a little closer to Callan and slipped her hand into his.

The building was imposing, and it was clearly luxurious living accommodation for high ranking officers.

She was a little afraid she'd be asked to leave before they reached their new home.

When the lift reached their floor without incident, the concierge gestured to the left, and they obediently started walking in that direction.

The apartment was only three down from the lift well, so before long, he was opening the door to let them in. "Welcome to your new home."

He handed Callan the key. "If you need anything, dial 9 for the front desk, and we'll arrange it for you."

Callan thanked him and slipped something into his hand before he turned and walked away.

They were left standing at the open door, hand in hand, looking down a brightly lit corridor into their new home.

"I'm a little nervous," she said.

He smiled, "me too, but maybe this will help."

He pulled her into his arms, and kissed her on the lips, before pulling back to look at her.

She was taken by surprise, but this was now a sanctioned relationship, and seeing him again had rekindled her crush.

She'd nothing to lose, just his love, respect, and care to gain.

Sera cupped his smooth cheek in her hand and looked up into his eyes for a long moment before kissing him back.

Callan groaned and crushed her body to his, before sweeping her off her feet and carrying her over the threshold.

《《 • 》》

The funny thing was though, while he'd visited other apartments in this building, he had no idea where the bedroom was in this one.

So he walked down the corridor to its end, where he gasped at the view of the sun setting over the City.

She slipped from his arms and walked towards the glass sliding doors separating them from the balcony, taking off her coat and throwing it on a nearby comfy chair.

The view of her back was as enticing as the first time he'd seen it, and her movements smooth and elegant as she removed her hat and jacket and threw them after the coat.

He struggled out of his coat, then stepped forward and wrapped his arms around her, leaning his chin on her shoulder to share the view.

She jumped, but leaned her head against his, "I've never seen anything as beautiful as this, have you?"

"No, it's breathtaking."

"I can't believe this is our new home. I thought it'd be a poky flat in The Shambles."

He smiled and kissed her neck, "I didn't think it would be that bad, but I think we can assume that the quality of our work has been rewarded with this residence."

She smiled and rubbed her face against his cheek, "I might be wrong, but I think I noticed a bottle of wine as you barged through the door."

He reluctantly let her go and backed away.

As he turned towards the room, he took off his cap and threw it on a chair, before sending his jacket and tie to follow.

His medals clinked gently as they landed.

He saw the wine chilling in an ice bucket, with two glasses on the dining table as he was rolling up his sleeves.

He poured the wine and brought it back to her, now leaning on the balcony handrail, glowing brighter than the dying sunlight.

"Here's to you, and a long and happy life together."

She blushed again, took the glass and clinked it against his, "no, here's to you."

He sat on a slatted wooden seat and patted the space next to him.

Sera looked at him for a moment, then kicked off her shoes and sat, curling up into his armpit.

He grunted as a hairpin dug into his underarm.

Putting his wine down, he started undoing her hair, gently pulling out a pin at a time.

Her breath quickened as he ran his fingers through it, drinking in its perfume until it was a river of fire down her back.

Pushing the weight of it aside, he kissed the nape of her neck and was rewarded when she turned to kiss him.

He thought he'd take it slow. They barely knew each other, and they had a long union ahead of them.

But then she slipped a hand between the buttons on his shirt.

Her fingers were still cool from the wine glass, and when they touched his hot skin, he knew he couldn't wait.

Taking her by the hand, he led her back into the apartment, throwing open door after door until he found the bedroom.

THE END

ALEXANDRIA BLAELOCK

AUTHOR OF FATE IN YOUR HANDS

SUCCESS AT THE ACADEMY

A SECURITY DIRECTORATE SHORT STORY

SUCCESS AT THE ACADEMY

Number 124 was spiteful.

But in the dog-eat-dog world of the State Academy of Cultural Regulation, that was a good thing.

There's no point in a Eugenics Programme that doesn't produce the citizens you're looking for.

Lieutenant Jemima Hunt blew her whistle, generating a breath of mist in the cold gymnasium air, and gestured for the boy to stand aside.

He stood slightly bent over, panting from his exertions, then started pacing a little to ease the muscle ache.

His underpants and singlet were his only protection from the cold, and after a good ten minutes of running hard on the treadmill, there was no sign of the goosebumps he'd walked in with.

She was warm enough in her thick blue tactical uniform, with her tiny medals lined up precisely across her left breast.

The smell of the child's fear tasted like acid on her tongue.

Understandable.

Failing any of the physical tests disqualified the children from all.

And by now, he and the other children knew any-one who failed, disappeared from school with no ex-planation.

There one day, gone the next. Never seen again.

Pale grey daylight leaked through the deep-set windows set high in the thick walls, but the bright electric lights suspended on long wires from the ceil-ing revealed the half-starved boy in all his pathetic scrawniness.

Though he was less emaciated than some of his classmates.

In a school that trained you to stand out rather than fit in, he was doing okay.

This physical assessment marked the end of his first year of basic training. A pass guaranteed promo-tion to the second year and a uniform issue.

Hopefully, he'd preserve a cool head; some kids got too cocky and failed out of their second year.

The key to surviving long enough to graduate was a slow, sustained effort. Just enough to make an im-pression on the teachers, but not so much to make yourself a target for the other kids.

Pass your physical, psychological, medical, and ac-ademic examinations, but not too well.

The skills the kids were developing as they dealt with each other, the over and underachieving stu-dents, and ensuring conformity amongst themselves, gave them a good grounding for their future careers.

If they did not get severely injured, stayed alive and passed their exams, their rewards were names and a place in the Protection Squadron.

But if, like her, they manifested some kind of useful genetic ability, known colloquially as a "superpower," they'd earn a placement at the University of Civilisation for Officer Training.

Though you never discussed your powers.

And if they graduated University, a Security Directorate Bureau career that made the best use of their abilities.

The gym echoed with the sound of movement. Whistles peeped, and voices barked as instructors walked, stacked heels thudding across the wooden floor. Children grunted and gasped with effort as they ran and jumped through the tests.

Hunt heard a loud crack behind her, and a child's scream quickly choked off.

It wasn't her candidate, so she didn't turn to look.

But the boy could see what happened, and his pale face took on a greenish tinge. She watched him swallow and stand a little straighter.

Good.

If he failed this physical assessment, like the injured child, the Bureau would divert him to the Euthanasia Programme, and that would be the last anyone would see of him.

It was a mercy really. There were no places in the Security Directorate for people who couldn't hold their own. No one was permitted to drain resources dedicated to the greater good.

She took the time and distance measurements from the treadmill and noted them on his assessment sheet, along with comments on his reaction to the injured child.

Too soon to know where 124 would end up, or even if he would live to see the end of his second year of training.

But with fewer students, he'd have greater access to food and resources, and his odds would improve.

Especially if he worked hard to develop his physical strength enough to access supplies allocated to other students.

The early signs were good, so Hunt was pretty sure he'd get there. One way or another.

A gurney cleared the injured child away, the proceed signal sounded, and Hunt gestured for 124 to precede her to the next testing station.

"Push-ups," she barked, setting the metronome at five seconds and starting her stopwatch.

He dropped to the floor with a thud and started doing push-ups, keeping up with the metronome reasonably well to start, though it wasn't that long until he fell behind. Nicely average between the best and worse recorded results.

She blew the whistle, and he stood aside, flicking his arms and legs out to ease them while she wrote his results on the assessment.

While they waited for the signal to move ahead, she watched him, trying not to fidget excessively.

There was something familiar about him, but she couldn't quite place it.

The next test was flexibility, some quick stretches to see where he fit.

Following her instructions, he demonstrated his shoulder mobility by reaching one hand over his shoulder and the other behind his back to clasp his hands.

He made it look easy. She checked a box.

Then he sat, legs fully extended and bent to hold his toes.

Easy. Another check.

He lay face down on the floor, arms held out to his side, and lifted his chest from the ground.

A little harder, but another check.

They seemed like simple tests, but these numbers would benchmark his results for the rest of his schooling. The school expected him to improve them as the years went by.

At the next station, she crouched to observe how high he could jump from standing. Three jumps, 15 seconds apart - just enough time to note the distance between jumps.

Slightly higher than average, but this gave him room to manoeuvre as he bulked up on his way through puberty.

Next, the penultimate test; endurance. The one that had earlier seen the end of the screaming child.

Just a grab bar you had to jump to reach, pull your chin above, then hold on tightly for as long as possible.

As if your life depended on it. Which in a way it did, though the children didn't know that.

124 frowned and licked his lips as he approached.

His little anxious face reminded her of her younger brother.

In a moment of weakness, she took pity on him and gave him an extra few seconds to pull himself together before she blew the whistle and started the stopwatch.

The second hand seemed to tick in slow motion as the boy grimaced, arms quivering, trying to hold on.

Tick.

Tick.

Tick.

He groaned and let go, landing neatly on both feet.

Good. Reasonable time. Clean landing. No injury.

Hunt nodded as she noted the time on the assessment form.

He rotated his arms backwards and forwards, seeking to ease the ache.

Was it possible they were related?

Like all children who passed their Genomics Bureau postnatal testing, the hospital had removed him from his parents and placed him in the State Academy. Almost from birth, he'd undertaken intensive education and physical training.

Learned about the Security Directorate and his potential place within it, as a Guardian of the Public Good.

In a few years, as his indoctrination continued, he'd learn more about how the machinery worked, and the sacrifices they all made to keep the Directorate strong.

Given her "superpower", it was inevitable. Sooner or later, she'd meet a family member on their way through the Academy.

That was why stripped the children of their identity and raised them in anonymity; to remove the possibility of nepotism or other bias during training and assessments.

Though it also functioned to break the bonds of family ties.

Only a few of the founding families claimed their kin when the names and families when revealed. And most graduates realised they'd managed well enough without family connections, so saw no reason to start familial relationships.

By this stage, 124 had more or less passed his physical assessment.

Hunt handed him the dynamometer and adjusted his grip on the device. "Hold tight for five seconds," she said, blew the whistle and started the stopwatch.

She gave him a 15-second break as she noted the weight. Another try, and another break. The last attempt.

Reasonable effort, within the range expected.

Time to evaluate his body.

She waved a hand at the height gauge, and he stood beneath it. She adjusted the bar and took the measurement.

He moved to stand on the weight scales and she noted his weight.

After a quick calculation, she added his body mass index.

She gestured for him to approach her, and when he did, pulled his singlet up.

He flinched at the touch of her icy fingers, but didn't squirm or try to evade her.

She pinched a fold of skin from his abdomen, clipped it with callipers, and noted the body fat measurement on his assessment sheet.

Doing well.

Last step, body measurements to check his body development and tailor his new school uniform.

"Arms out."

She picked a tape measure up and checked his shoulder, chest, waist, arm and leg length and circumference.

As she wrote his measurements on the form, she snuck glances over her clipboard.

Of course, it was possible they were related.

She counted back to her prenatal confinement and looked at him again.

It was possible he was her son.

She hadn't taken his removal well.

The Genomics Bureau had extended her postnatal confinement while they monitored her condition. And increased her drug doses.

She'd felt his loss keenly, but that was just one of many sacrifices she'd made for the Greater Good.

If you wanted to live, you adapted and moved on.

She hadn't contested when her husband petitioned the Genomics Bureau to end their contract early.

She didn't blame him.

Given the events surrounding the birth, it was unlikely that she'd be paired with anyone else.

Unfortunate, but expected.

Hunt nodded her dismissal of 124 and pointed toward the exit door.

He bowed formally, turned smartly, and marched from the room.

Jemima clutched the clipboard to her chest and watched him leave before writing some notes on her general impressions of him, his attitude, and abilities.

She signed his sheet, passing his first physical examination of his basic training, granting him a promotion to second year.

Effectively authorising his continued existence.

Until the next assessment.

His life was about to get a lot more complicated than it already was. But at least it was a new life.

She looked up at the ceiling as she remembered the dormitory she'd grown up in. Bare concrete walls, cold concrete floors. A small steel bed frame next to a small steel locker.

The bare minimum of comforts to build strong characters.

Some kid from the country had smuggled a flower in and left in on her locker. She'd turned him in after she'd beaten him up.

Her single teacher's room was not so very different from the children's dormitories.

And these days she'd welcome a flower.

Even a dandelion.

Maybe it was time to apply to the Genomics Bureau and see what they had to offer.

It might be nice to be with someone.

To once again be someone's beloved.

THE END

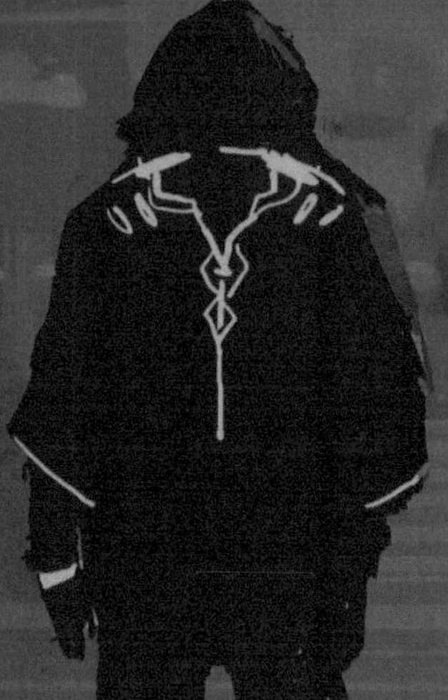

ALEXANDRIA
BLAELOCK
AUTHOR OF FATE IN YOUR HANDS
PAYTON'S
RUN
A SECURITY DIRECTORATE SHORT STORY

PAYTON'S RUN

Payton finished retying her shoelaces, and not for the first time queried the necessity of heeled walking shoes.

There was no doubt they were strikingly elegant. Perhaps a little intimidating, in combination with the navy blue tactical uniform of kick pleated pencil skirt suit.

But not necessarily practical.

Which was of course why you wore the uniform for all physical training classes.

After graduation, you were always on duty, and never knew when you'd need to chase someone down.

If you wanted to maintain your authority in all circumstances, you had to adapt to the uniform's limitations so completely you could safely react in an instant.

No one respects or fears a woman in a torn skirt, and you needed people to look up to you, not down on you.

Her fitted jacket absorbed the warmth of the sun, releasing the odour of dry cleaning chemicals.

Which was, of course, the other downside of physical training - the cost of keeping your uniform clean and fresh was astronomical.

Some students cheated and saved one jacket just for the physical classes, but she was a little too fastidious for that.

Not to mention you never knew when the Generals would make a surprise inspection and they frowned on that kind of sloppiness.

The uniform was a symbol of the Protection Squadron's ultimate power, to be treated with reverence, and cared for properly.

Lest you find yourself on the wrong side of it.

Improper dress was one of many ways to pick up demerit points. If you accrued enough of them, you'd be expelled from the University of Civilisation.

And despite having passed the Genomics Bureau post-natal testing, and surviving the State Academy of Cultural Regulation, expulsion was the end of your high-level career.

The Directorate didn't permit rogues with the kind of genetic abilities known colloquially as "superpowers" to go free.

If you were "lucky", you'd be forcibly lobotomised, and get a place in the lower ranks of the Protection Squadron. Your life would be short, but you'd be taken care of.

If you weren't lucky, you'd be shunted into the euthanasia programme, and that would be the end of you.

Payton closed her eyes and turned to face the sun. Its warmth offset the cool breeze, and it was a pleasant day.

The kind of day normals would go for country walks, picnics or punting on the river.

No such luxury for her.

Her physical final was fast approaching, and a lot was riding on it.

There were no second chances; if she failed the physical, she'd fail her course, and wouldn't graduate.

It would be the end of her career.

Payton marched onto the freshly mown sports ground. She smoothed her skirt across her hips, checked to make sure all her jacket buttons were secured and adjusted the placement of her hat.

Then she checked her practice firearm was loaded with pellets, and the safety was on.

She couldn't just scrape a pass in the physical exam either, the physical prowess and endurance she demonstrated had a direct bearing on her first and future placements.

Which made the stakes higher, because physical training was not one of her better subjects.

Despite the weight training, her slight physique made it difficult to cope with some of the physical obstructions.

But it was useful for escape scenarios and encouraged other people to underestimate her abilities.

Plus, she'd learned to leverage her body weight and strength for advantage in hand-to-hand combat.

She made it look easy, but it was gruelling work.

Having completed a lap of the oval, she stood on the grass to complete her warm-up.

Standing, with her feet shoulder-width apart, she rotated her head across her shoulders, grunting a little as her stiff neck protested from the pain of crouching over her desk for the last few weeks cramming for her academic finals.

She rotated her shoulder joints backwards and forwards, followed by her elbows, wrists, hips, knees and ankles.

Then some dynamic stretches, focusing on stretching her arms and wrists to their maximum, hamstrings, bending from the hips to touch her toes, and finishing with some lunges.

As she stretched, she reflected that while her uniform was restrictive, it did offer the practical benefits of compression and leverage.

Maybe that was the key lesson of the physical component, learning how to make the best use of the limited materials that were available to you.

And why no additional protective gear was permitted during the exercises; it was unlikely they'd be available to you during the usual course of your duties.

With her warm-up complete, she took a deep breath and used her University identification card to swipe into the training village.

She walked down the main street, carefully observing the terrain.

It had once been a vibrant local community, but during the Bread Riots decades earlier, the surviving villagers had been driven out and not permitted to return.

Sounds harsh, but alive and hungry is better than dead and dead.

The village had been left to deteriorate until the University acquired the land for Urban Warfare training.

Automated training exercises included both offensive and defensive manoeuvres, and she'd booked both for her hour-long session.

While she'd been through the village several times, the physical and holographic hazards were programmed to randomly activate according to what you were doing to provide a semi-realistic scenario.

There would be targets that flipped and ran, there might be weather events, collapsing buildings or explosions.

And as a final year student, the safety would be off, so she'd be facing live ammunition with the real possibility of injury or even death.

Payton was comfortable with the risk, she wouldn't be training otherwise.

And she did enjoy the combination of intellectual analysis and gut instinct, and hoped her first job would involve a placement where she could use these skills.

As she strolled, seemingly unconcerned down the footpath close to the buildings, her navy uniform melted into the shadows.

She looked in the windows, assessing the reflected environment for unusual signs of movement, listened for sounds, and sniffed for odours that might indicate an attack.

As a Protection Squadron Officer, there was always a fine line between her presence as a visible deterrent/target and the need for covert operations.

Something flashed to her left, and she ducked to reduce her target size.

She heard footsteps running down the street, but there was no tell-tale aroma of gunfire. Whoever was running hadn't fired a shot. Was it a lure drawing her into a trap, or someone fleeing from the sight of her uniform?

She quickly scanned the street, noting it was quiet and clear.

The overpass further down could obstruct her line of sight, offering the potential of an ambush.

She looked up at the building she was sheltering below and thought the third story window offered a good sniper position with the correct trajectory for a kill shot near the overpass.

Payton didn't think she'd survive the overpass and chose to enter the building to clear the possible sniper.

She withdrew her weapon and eased slowly through the door, giving her eyes time to adjust to the gloom inside.

Clearing the room would be quicker and easier with an assault team, but she had no choice but to proceed alone.

She'd have to carefully weigh each decision.

The foyer appeared clear, so she turned left towards the staircase.

It was on the external wall, with light streaming through the tall, slightly opaque safety glass windows.

She glanced up to see a solid roof and understood she could be attacked only from front and rear.

Senses straining, trying to avoid silhouetting herself against the windows, she rapidly climbed from the ground to the third floor and approached the sniper's nest.

Hearing a faint sigh, she spun around, but the target was a secretary with a stack of files. She pointed it back towards the office it came from, and it slid obediently away.

The slight movement was enough to warn the sniper, and a volley of shots broke out.

Payton dropped to the floor, rolled onto her stomach and crawled closer to the door.

At that moment it flew open, and a holographic sniper ran from the room, she rolled and shot up at it until it fell.

She checked it was dead before entering the room to find it empty.

That was the first target secured.

Before leaving, she stood beside the window, looking down the street for other potential hazards and found none.

It seemed safe to proceed.

But she was running out of time.

As she retreated to the stairs, she decided to go up rather than down.

At the top, she found a small door out onto the roof, and opening it a crack, looked down over the grey rooftops and terracotta chimney pots.

There were no readily identifiable hazards, it was a beautiful day, and the village looked charming from above, so she decided to finish with a race across the rooftops.

She chose to avoid the church and make directly for the exit, so the rest of her session passed relatively uneventfully.

She ran lightly across the rooftops, somersaulting across gaps between buildings, and sliding down the ridgelines.

Now and again, there was a potshot from the street below or a passing thug target to shoot down.

Occasionally, just for fun, she'd flip and run up or down a wall.

After exiting the village, she stopped outside the Debriefing Centre to do some static stretches and shake out her limbs to cool down her tired muscles.

Then went inside, washed her face and tidied her hair before reviewing her performance.

"Nice job Cadet," said the officer in attendance, exchanging her practice firearm for a restorative drink and her assessment print out.

"If you have any questions, come back to me".

She nodded, took the paper and drink to a table where she sat and read the report.

She'd taken a few minutes more than an hour to complete the course.

Not too bad, though if you didn't exit on time, you risked being caught up in, and graded for someone else's exercise.

She'd "killed" all the essential targets along her route, "spared" the right number of civilians, used a reasonable amount of ammunition to achieve her objectives.

All in all, not too bad, though it was hard to know how useful that exercise would be for her final.

It didn't feel like she'd done much, but her body and brain were tired, and she wanted a hot shower.

There'd be enough time for a recovery nap before dinner.

She adjusted the set of her uniform and nodded at the officer as she left the building.

It was a long walk, uphill, around the village back to the dorm, so there was plenty of time to consider the physical final.

All she knew, was that now her final written and oral exams were over, the physical would take place sometime during the next two weeks.

The scenario was tailored to your individual strengths and weaknesses. The Directorate's goal, to expose any impediments to the potential careers that had been plotted for you.

It might be a hostage rescue, taking down a criminal kingpin or stealing an item of significance.

It would be a live scenario through an inhabited area, relying only on her physical abilities, no superpowers permitted.

During the event, she'd endure various armed and unarmed assaults, and was expected to achieve her objective without harming any citizens.

If she were injured or killed, she'd fail.

If she didn't capture her target, she'd fail.

If she harmed innocent citizens, she'd fail.

She wouldn't know who, if anyone, she could trust or rely on.

The prospect was terrifying, but theoretically, she had all the skills she needed.

And while her recent exercise had been uneventful, perhaps that indicated good strategic thinking.

No matter what else happened, it was best to minimise the risks to herself and others as much as possible and come out at the end unharmed.

Even if it felt like cheating.

She was caught off guard when someone grabbed her from behind, pinning her arms to her body, and roughly pulling a bag over her head.

Her mind went blank, and she froze for an instant, but it was long enough to be bundled into a vehicle, and hear the back doors slam.

She couldn't tell how many men were in the van, or what language they were speaking, but her struggled attempt to break free and escape was met with a solid punch to the guts that took the wind out of her.

Someone banged on the wall.

The engine roared, and tyres squealed as the vehicle started moving.

They took advantage of her weakness to start taping up her wrists, but while she couldn't breathe or fight, her brain had kicked in.

She let her hands fall open as she crossed her wrists to maximise their size and leave some room to break the tape.

As her captors moved to tape her ankles, she tensed them to increase their size and held them a little apart so that tape would also be a little loser.

As she caught her gasping breath, she started sobbing, and they laughed derisively.

As if in response, she rolled to face the wall of the van and curled protectively around her belly.

They seemed to think she was defeated, and aside from a half-hearted kick let her be.

They huddled somewhere nearby discussing something, but the tones of their voices didn't suggest she was in immediate danger.

The most likely scenario was being taken to a secondary location for interrogation or ransom.

Or maybe both.

Whatever their plans, she needed to set herself free before they reached it.

As she started taking stock of her situation, one of the men lit a cigarette, while another made a joke and they all laughed.

So, she was in a closed compartment with three men. The driver was not in it with them and would need to be dealt with separately.

The door was at her feet, and it used a latch mechanism.

She was fully dressed, lying on some sort of rough fabric, hands and feet bound.

Her hands were bound in front of her.

If she was relatively still, they might interpret her movements as swaying with the vehicle rather than attempting to free herself.

The hood was still on her head, but the weave was loose and she could discern shapes, and probably movement around her.

The smooth ride and sound of the tyres suggested an asphalt road, and the frequent pauses, acceleration and deceleration suggested they were driving on City streets.

The best option seemed to be freeing herself before the vehicle left the confines of the City.

That meant freeing her feet and getting out the vehicle were the critical tasks.

Once she was running, she could free her hands, lose herself in the crowds of citizens, and make her way back to campus.

And the quickest way to do that was to leave her hat behind and unpin her hair.

Demerit points be dammed!

While she didn't have a firearm, she did have a razor blade concealed in the heel of her shoe.

And at this moment, trussed up in this van, she was grateful the heels offered her more than a slim calf and sexy stance.

Though it wasn't going to be easy to get at them. Should have practised more in her spare time.

Another joke suggested her guards were amateurs, and wouldn't be carefully watching her.

She risked bending further to reach her feet while at the same time nodding her head a little in time to the vehicle's movements to loosen her hat and partially roll up the hood.

So far, so good.

She managed to get the blade free and cut the tape but didn't kick it off immediately. At a glance, it would look secure, yet be easy to kick off when the time came.

In the meantime, she carefully tucked the blade between the fingers of her right hand in case she needed it as a weapon.

Still gently moving her head, she dislodged her hat. If she sat up rapidly, the weight of it should pull the hood off so she could see what she was doing.

Her captors were still talking, and she hadn't heard anything to suggest there were weapons so it might be possible to get a second or two ahead of them.

Now that she'd worked through a scenario, she was ready to put it into action.

The vehicle slowed, and she tensed her muscles.

When the vehicle stopped, she sat up rapidly losing the hood.

Then she leaned forward, dug one heel into the floor and leveraged herself into a crouch from which she could open the door with her bound hands.

As she half fell, half stepped out of the vehicle, she quickly assessed the new environment.

There were shops nearby, with plenty of civilians coming and going.

There was a large department store a little further down the street, so she started to run towards it.

As she ran, she lifted her hands and abruptly pulled them down towards her abdomen, using her body as a wedge to tear the tape open.

She heard the men shouting behind her, and a few shots fired, but made it to the store unharmed.

She bolted inside, tearing the pins out of her hair, and fluffing it up, so her waist-length locks hung freely down her back.

Aware that they'd be looking for someone in uniform running, she headed towards the centre of the ground floor, unbuttoning her jacket and blouse.

As she passed a display table, she grabbed a bright floral scarf and wound it around her neck.

Moving past another, she added some jangly bracelets for her wrists.

She took a large flower pin from a third and pinned it in her hair as she picked up a brightly coloured handbag from a fourth.

Then layered in a generous spray of an intense oriental fragrance on her way to the makeup counter.

She snatched up cosmetics here and there and applied them thickly.

As she turned to inspect herself in the mirror, she was rudely pushed out of the way by a man in rough tradesman clothing and a baseball cap.

Was he one of her kidnappers?

She continued sauntering through the ground floor towards an exit on the other side.

The security guard looked like he was going to arrest her, so she flashed her Protection Squadron identification, and he stood down.

She debated for a moment whether to inform him of the kidnappers, but decided that would waste valuable escape time.

She'd be better able to access her memories under interrogation back at the University anyway.

She nodded at the guard and left the store, just in time to jump on a bus heading towards the University.

Taking a seat, she closed her eyes for a moment in relief at having escaped.

Seemingly safe, but still on edge.

She thought she heard shouting, but didn't risk turning to see what the commotion was about.

It was several stops before she could relax enough to slump in the seat and take some long slow breaths to dissipate the tension in her neck and shoulders.

Arriving back at the University, she wasn't exactly sure whether to report the kidnapping immediately or clean up first.

But the decision was taken out of her hands by the arrival of campus police.

"Ma'am, you're out of uniform, please follow us to the Disciplinary Unit."

Payton nodded assent and fell in.

Now that she was back on campus, she was more than happy to let someone else take the lead.

In any case, she was too tired to argue, and at least this way she'd get something to drink and her interrogation would be over sooner.

The officer escorted her through the door and gestured towards an interview room.

"Please wait in here Ma'am," he said, opening the door and closing it behind her.

She set the stolen bag on the table, then removed the rest of her disguise piece by piece, folding it carefully and laying it out in a row.

She was attempting to secure her hair when the door opened, and her academic supervisor entered.

She dropped her hair and saluted smartly.

"Congratulations Lieutenant, you've passed both your academic and physical examinations and are approved for graduation."

She broke into a wide grin as he pulled a small box from his pocket and continued, "I'm authorised to pin your official insignia to your uniform."

He unbuttoned and removed the unadorned shoulder boards from her jacket, and replaced them with her new one pip boards, before taking a step back and saluting.

She returned his salute.

"Your orders will arrive in the next few days, so in the meantime, relax and celebrate before the hard work begins."

THE END

ALEXANDRIA BLAELOCK

AUTHOR OF FATE IN YOUR HANDS

MINTY AND THE MONSTER

A SECURITY DIRECTORATE SHORT STORY

MINTY AND THE MONSTER

Apparently, the cave was magical.

At least if you believed in that kind of thing.

And newly graduated second Lieutenant Minty Hollister definitely did not believe in magic.

A Eugenics Programme success, she'd passed the Genomics Bureau post-natal testing, survived the State Academy of Cultural Regulation with a useful genetic "superpower" and graduated from the University of Civilisation.

She *knew* she was the one who made magic.

Not the traditional abracadabra kind of magic. Her genetic "superpower" was the ability to get inside people's heads to discover their dreams, the ones they didn't know they had.

And then she made it feel like they'd come true.

It was a different kind of magic entirely, even if it was just the kind that involved a fistful of glitter.

And the Cabaret Cave renovation was the magical triumph of dream infused marketing hype.

Not that all dreams were so concrete or permanent. And not that they didn't come and go according to the fortunes of each minute of every day.

Standing in the artfully reconstructed wilderness outside the main entrance, Minty tried, one-handed, to poke some loose hair back into her regulation chignon. Failing charmingly, she clutched her clipboard and prepared to enter the cave.

If anything went wrong at the inaugural Distinguished Service Awards dinner, her career would be over before it had begun.

The job of a glorified party planner was not what she'd had in mind as she'd worked her way through the University of Civilisation.

But the Authorities supposedly allocated work placements on the basis of your powers and grades, so she had to wonder. Was this her ideal calling, had she messed up big-time, or was this just one small step on the way to something more significant?

Though in some ways, the transitory nature of event planning was its own reward. Like a magic trick that surprises you for an instant, and leaves you wondering how the magician did it for a long time after.

A brief, but intense experience that seemingly changed the world forever.

And while Chef Joshua Richards was the Cave's Commandant, in charge of personnel discipline and welfare, she was now in charge of operations at this beautiful venue, so she couldn't really complain too much.

Even though she was terrified of messing it up.

They'd fenced the wide mouth of the cave in wrought iron with a beautifully large and strangely hypnotic, sinuous vine motif. The centrally located gates folded back to reveal a gentle slope down into the side of the mountain.

From this vantage point, the wide path seemed smooth, which was just as well, because the glistening limestone formations were stunningly distracting. Huge folds of warm red, ochre and brown stalactite drapery hung from the ceiling. Stalagmite columns rose from the ground, and flowstone waterfalls fell from outcroppings in the walls.

Closing her mouth, she tore her gaze from the roof and focused on the ground. Pulling a small torch from her pocket, she played the light across the ground looking for trip hazards.

Discrete lights focused on the formations along the way; garlands of flowers, an elephant, and an old man's face, among others. Not bright enough to damage them, but bright enough to cast enough light to walk down the path without faltering.

It looked good. She put the torch away, pulled a cute, glittery cat topped pen from behind her ear and ticked a box on her checklist.

So far, so good. It looked a lot like the image she'd plucked from the Deputy Director-General's mind.

And she really hoped she never had to do that again - the man's mind was a nightmare vision of possibility.

After leaving his office, she'd had to take a quick trip to the bathroom to vomit up the nastiness she'd seen.

Unfortunately, not as easy to forget, especially standing in the middle of his dream come true project.

How could someone who could dream up something as pretty as this could also dream up so much nastiness?

As she descended further, phantasms from the Deputy Director-General's head were all around her and failing someone whose superpower was to remove nastiness, an industrial-strength psy-vacuum would be the next best thing.

Only she wasn't entirely sure that either of those things actually existed.

The calming, and pleasantly earthy smell of mud rose to meet her as she descended. The drainage channels by the side of the path seemed to do their jobs and earned a tick.

The cave's interior grew cooler, but compared to the heat outside, it was comfortable. The depth should ensure it seemed comfortably warm in winter too.

She paused before the glass doors to the cave foyer, and growled as she shook herself like a dog to dissipate the Deputy Director-General's residual negative energy before entering.

The renovations had left the fundamental structure of the cave intact. They'd coated the concrete piers supporting the roof in a gritty resin mixture to resemble more natural formations, so the transition from resin to roof was almost imperceptible.

She nodded and added a tick to the list.

The earth-coloured terrazzo floor had settled nicely level and unbroken on the ground. With the top layer polished back to a fine shine, it looked as if the floor was speckled with gold dust.

And it probably was.

Another tick on the list.

Minty took a quick trip through the bathrooms, admiring the redwood cubicles, turning on all the chrome-plated taps, and flushing all the white porcelain sanitary ware. Plenty of soft paper goods and lightly citrus-scented soap in the dispensers.

She looked in the spotless mirror and tried to adjust her hair again. It was like it had a life of its own, completely independent of her.

"What do you want?" she asked it.

"What do *you* want?" her echo replied.

A lock fell loose from behind her ear.

It seemed her hair wanted to be free.

She sighed and left it where it was as she turned to survey the room one last time. It was entirely possible the luxury finishes would make a trip to the facilities a highlight of the evening. If not the highlight.

For those who didn't win, anyway.

Tick, tick, tick, and tick.

The cloakroom sported a curved reception counter in the same redwood, and across the top of it, she saw rows of wooden lockers of various sizes, each with a small numbered chrome tag hanging from the door. Minty walked through the room, giving each row a cursory glance, on guard for ugliness.

From a guest perspective, all good, another tick.

Depending on the function size and number of attendants, it would probably be a nightmarish place to work, but that wasn't her problem.

Actually, it kind of was, but she couldn't do anything about it. And none of the Senior Officers cared about the "goons" anyway.

She, on the other hand, did.

In her eyes, the fact that the Privates hadn't shown "useful" powers at the Academy of Cultural Regulation didn't make them any less human. Not to mention that someone had to take out the trash.

And as they were the steel spine of the Protection Squad, it was at least appropriate to treat them with courtesy, and address them by rank the same as Officers.

Just past the cloakroom was a board with the seating plan, beside a small white-clothed table ready to be laid out with glasses of champagne as the guests arrived.

And just past that, the main function room entrance was through an artfully constructed rockfall. It looked entirely natural, even inspecting it closely, and she wondered whether they'd blown a hole to make it.

Surely not.

Would they?

She diligently ticked another box on her checklist.

All the overhead lights shone steadily and silently; another tick.

Ten round tables danced around an open space in the middle of the room. Each had ten chairs (check), white tablecloths (check), and laid with white and silver-coloured settings for ten (check). An arrangement of yellow roses sat within a silver candelabra in the centre, one condiment set on either side (check).

She leaned over to examine the flowers at the closest table. They were fresh, unmarked, and unscented. Almost too perfect to be the real (and expensive) flowers she knew they were.

Were they "natural" or did someone have a superpower that produced perfect flowers?

She walked across the dance floor to the small raised dais on the other side. Her heels clicked smartly on the terrazzo but barely echoed in the large room.

She climbed the stairs to find the small stage was neat and clean, furnished only with a lectern and flag-covered table ready to receive the medals.

She stood behind the lectern and switched on the power. The tiny reading lamp flickered on, and as the computer powered up, the teleprompters reflected the text of the first speech back at the lectern. Hopefully already adjusted for the height of the Awards host.

Putting her clipboard down, she held the edges of the lectern in both hands and looked out over the tables and imaginary seated diners. It felt like a position of power. All those people looking expectantly up at her.

It made her uncomfortable and excited at the same time. This felt like the place where one small step at the wrong time would send your life in a different direction entirely.

Or maybe the right time.

She could almost feel a multitude of different lives spilling out from her as the seconds passed.

The symmetrically organised main floor looked good from this vantage point, so she cleared her throat and signalled the Private in charge of lighting. He obediently flicked a switch.

The room plunged momentarily into darkness, before the strings of tiny golden lights set into the walls and ceiling silently lit up like a billion stars.

Or given it was a cave, fireflies.

Or if you wanted to keep the magic theme going, like fairies.

After a moment, when the globes had adequately warmed up, and they started flickering at seemingly random intervals.

The effect was really beautiful, and for a moment, Minty was stabbed by bitter envy of the Directorate Officers who would attend the Awards Dinner that evening.

Partly because they would be guests enjoying the just rewards of their hard work, and partly because it was ever so unlikely that anyone ever from the Propaganda Bureau would ever attend an Awards dinner to receive a Distinguished Service Medal.

Let alone her.

Or get to wear a long, sparkly, swishy dress. Maybe something in a lime green.

Though technically any event she went to (ever) would be in her black dress uniform, not a long, sparkly swishy dress. Which was a shame, because no matter what anyone said, black was just not her colour.

But like every other Directorate Officer, she couldn't use her superpower on herself. Which, as far as everyone else was concerned, was probably a good thing, otherwise the world would drown in glitter.

Not that dreams came true with no obvious effort on the dreamer's part, but it would have been nice to have a clear path to follow.

Even if it was knee-deep in glitter.

Though that's probably how she'd know it was the right path anyway, because it was strewn with glitter.

Maybe it was worth keeping a lookout for glitter where she least expected it.

But in the meantime, back to the job at hand.

She scratched the back of her neck with slightly longer than regulation fingernails and ticked a bunch of boxes on her checklist.

A quick check of her watch revealed it was T minus five hours.

"Private," she said, partly to test the sound.

"Ma'am," he said as he saluted.

"You may stand down. Please put the overheads back on, and be ready to resume your duties at 17:00 hours."

"Ma'am."

He switched the lights, saluted, then turned on his heel and left the room.

"Thank you, Private."

She turned off the lectern, ticked a few more boxes, and that was the function room cleared.

Stifling the temptation to thoroughly scratch her head with both hands, she took off her cap and used the cat end of her pen to scratch the top of it, dislodging a little more hair.

She knew this jittery, itchy feeling was just apprehension, and that it would subside once the event started. In the meantime, she just had to ignore it as best she could and keep going.

Putting her cap back on, she turned towards the operational side of the cave and walked down the service corridor to the kitchens.

A few Privates had started the food preparation, and something deliciously savoury already scented the air.

The office door was open, revealing Chef at his desk, so she knocked on the door frame.

He nodded toward her and stood as she took a couple of steps into the room and saluted, dislodging a few specks of glitter onto her shoulder.

He smiled, almost imperceptibly, "at ease Lieutenant."

She relaxed slightly, "thank you Chef. Just checking the renovations meet your requirements?"

"They completed the kitchens to my specifications, and all appliances are operating satisfactorily."

She nodded and ticked off a few items on the checklist, "do you have all the staff and supplies you need?"

He glanced at his watch, "all staff have received their commissions, and are familiar with the venue. We've made a practice run, and have all the equipment we need."

She nodded again and added some ticks and notes on her checklist.

"You flew in from your previous post this morning?"

"Yes Sir."

"Have you eaten?"

"No Sir."

He stepped past her, out of this office and shouted, "Jones."

"Yes Chef!"

"The soup please."

"Yes Chef!" the Private, picked up a wire basket containing a small vacuum flask and a bowl with a bread roll in it and brought it over.

"Thank you Private," Chef said, and took the basket. He nodded and walked back to his station.

Minty was momentarily stunned by Chef's politeness, though she supposed the kitchen was an intensely intimate working space with different relational norms to the usual.

She'd read his profile, and it suggested he was not just well-respected, but well-liked too.

"Your trunk arrived yesterday, and the maid service has unpacked for you. Your dress uniform is cleaned and pressed, so you're good to go for this evening."

Which was unexpected as well as kind. She hadn't been looking forward to trying to press her uniform before the event.

"I'll show you to your quarters. You can take a break for an hour or two to rest and have a snack before the evening gets going."

And as soon as he said it, she suddenly felt tired, and a nap sounded like the best idea ever.

She drooped a little as she followed him out of the kitchen and down a warren of corridors.

While she'd memorised the floor plan, she was quickly disoriented, and was relieved to see the Directorate standard coloured navigation strips on the walls.

At least knowing the address of her rooms, she'd be able to find her way until she knew the place better.

He opened the door and walked through a small secretarial office furnished with the same redwood and chrome fixtures as the function rooms, smelling of leather and cigar smoke.

Through a solid wood door to a more spacious main office in the same style.

Her jaw dropped at the size and luxuriousness; she was very conscious of its polished perfection in contrast to her own nebulous loosey goosiness.

Was all this just for her?

Probably not.

The décor must be more about those seeking a once in a lifetime event than her. Something imposing and awe-inspiring that would make Directorate Officers feel appropriately cared for.

But as she turned, trying to take it all in, she noticed a few small specks of gold in the terrazzo floor and was comforted.

Anyway, after a point, she'd probably wouldn't even notice the décor.

Chef put the basket on the desk, then handed her the key. "I'll leave you to rest. The guests will start arriving at 18:00, so please call past the kitchen around 17:00, so I know you're up and okay."

"Thank you Sir."

As he shut the door behind him, she threw her cap on the desk and dug her fingers into her scalp for a good hard scratch. Pins plinked to the floor as her hair unravelled, but she ignored them.

Through a door hidden in a bookshelf, she accessed a corridor containing a kitchenette on one side, and an enclosed bathroom on the other. She stopped to use the facilities, barely noticing the same high-quality fixtures as the public bathrooms at the entry.

She yawned as she went through to the last room in the suite; the bedroom. An enormous bed, crisp white bedding, and a vase of perfect, highly scented yellow roses on a chest of drawers.

Though who they thought she'd be entertaining in here was a matter to think about another day.

After travelling halfway around the world in the last thirty-six hours, she abruptly ran out of backup power and was asleep almost before her fully clothed body hit the bed.

《《 • 》》

Minty stood at ease in the entry foyer. To the Privates stationed here and there, she appeared calm and serene, but she was as nervous as all hell and itched all over.

Nothing to do with her immaculate uniform, or the soft citrus-scented soap she'd bathed with, just the usual pre-event jitters.

There was a rumour the Director General himself would be in attendance. It seemed unlikely, and she wasn't sure whether she hoped he would or wouldn't.

She wasn't supposed to read people without their permission, and generally wore gloves to prevent it, but sometimes a little something got through when she couldn't control her excitement. Or perhaps they couldn't conceal theirs.

What would his dreams be like?

She remembered the nastiness of his deputy's mind and swallowed with apprehension.

Of course, he wouldn't be here.

As the first guests approached the main door, she glided to meet them, inviting them to check their coats, showing them the seating plan, and suggesting they take a glass of champagne with them as they entered the function room.

As more and more guests arrived, a couple of Privates joined in greeting and directing, and she relaxed a little and backed off.

She started picking up some excitement about hurting someone important. It was rare that she'd pick up broadcasts with so much clarity, and it made her suspicious.

She started circulating among the guests, ostensibly checking they had a drink and knew where they were sitting, but really to see if she could pick up the person dreaming of harm.

And of course, she did.

It was a dreary little man, slightly balding, with a ridiculously luxurious moustache, some kind of adjutant. Presumably to the tall, distinguished man in the unmarked, black dress uniform.

Unmarked, as in no rank marked epaulettes, as if no one needed to know exactly who it was.

Minty focused on the man, and as he turned and she saw his face, she realised, of course, he didn't need rank insignia.

She'd studied under his benevolent gaze at the Academy, and pledged him her allegiance at the University every day.

It was THE Director General.

Was he aware he harboured a viper in his chest?

Not that she needed to worry. A discreet glance around the room revealed his Officers installed in strategic locations.

She glanced around for Chef, but of course, he'd be busy in the kitchens.

As the Commandant, presumably, the Director General had already seen him or would meet him after the meal.

And presumably, the DG's guys were on top of things. But even assuming his guys were on his side, they were looking for general risks. It was unlikely they'd be looking at his closest aides as threats.

There was no way she was going to let something happen to the DG on her watch. She didn't see an opportunity to approach the adjutant, let alone take off her gloves and touch his bare skin. But, for her own peace of mind, she needed to at least set a couple of her guys to watch him.

Except she'd just arrived, and didn't know any of them yet. She scanned the room, looking for someone familiar, and spotted the Private of the lights from the afternoon.

She looked at her watch and walked smartly over to him as if to issue instructions, which she was, but she hoped it would appear to relate to the function, not the DG. He stiffened to attention as she stopped in front of him.

She nodded. "Private, do you see the small man with the big moustache behind me, next to the Director General?"

"Yes Ma'am."

"Would you please choose someone else from your unit and keep an eye on him?"

"Yes Ma'am. Are we looking for something in particular?"

"I'm not sure. He's just giving off a weird vibe. Look for something odd that's not in keeping with attendance at an awards dinner."

"Yes Ma'am."

She turned to walk away, but turned her head back to look at him, "be prepared to use force Private."

"Yes Ma'am."

They walked in opposite directions.

Okay.

The DG had people looking after him, and she had people watching the adjutant. What was next?

Well, next was doing her job.

And that was getting people into the function room and seated at their tables so the event could proceed. She wanted the winners still mostly sober when they collected their awards.

Officers or not, it was going to get messy later.

She focused on rounding up the guests and encouraging them to sit at their allocated tables.

Another quick watch check and she sent a Private to signal delivery of the first course. And not long after, giving the Colonel Master of Ceremonies the go-ahead to start proceedings.

Minty stood in the background, in a corner of the room, not listening to what they said, but watching for mini-disasters in the making. Just the little things like allergic reactions, uniform failures, and cutlery drops. Just trying to keep the evening light and happy.

She saw the adjutant get up and leave the room, and pulled off her gloves as she started following him. She noticed her Private moving to intercept as well and was relieved there would be someone to assist.

She caught up with him as he left the room, and breaking protocol, grabbed his hand.

He tried to pull it free as he turned to confront her, but she kept hold of it as long as she could, asking "is everything okay Sir? Can I help you with something?"

"I'm fine," he snapped. "I'm just heading to the bathroom."

But she already knew he was trying to leave the cave because there was a bomb in a locker in the cloakroom.

It was set to go off in thirty minutes.

And if she didn't do something about it, the whole place would go up.

She checked the time and took the locker tag from his pocket, hoping his power wasn't something that would interfere with her preventing the explosion.

"Private, please secure the adjutant in the brig, and ask Chef to join me in the cloakroom immediately."

"Ma'am." He and his colleague dragged the struggling adjutant away down a side corridor where he wouldn't disturb the proceedings.

She thought she remembered seeing someone from the Bomb Squad on the guest list and double-checked the seating plan. There he was, Major Matthews, a nominee in the Outstanding Bravery category.

Apt.

She ducked inside and asked him to step outside for a moment.

He obliged. She closed the function room doors behind him, and picking up the relevant key, led him to the locker.

"Major, there's a bomb in here, and it's set to go off in about twenty-five minutes.

"As the bomber didn't place it himself, I'm pretty sure it's safe to open the locker door.

"Would you please examine it and tell me if you can defuse it in time, or if I need to evacuate the caves?"

He nodded, took the key, and opened the door.

She took a couple of steps back and bumped into Chef.

"Commandant," she started, but he waved her away.

"I've been here long enough to get the gist of it."

They waited as Major Matthews hummed to himself and delicately probed the device.

"I can disable it, but I'll need some sticks, clamps, pliers, a small Phillips screwdriver, and snips."

The Private had returned unnoticed, "Sir, I've been studying for my disposals certificate and have an Explosive Ordinance Kit Level 2 as well as a bomb suit if you'd like to use it?"

"Thanks son, run along and grab it quickly."

He turned to Minty and Chef, "It's a fairly amateur attempt, and I believe I can disable it before it goes off. Should only take five minutes or so once I've got the gear."

Minty looked at her watch, "there's twenty minutes remaining, is that enough of a margin?"

He frowned and looked up at the ceiling, "probably."

She looked at Chef, "What do you think Sir, evacuate or not?"

The Private slid the last few metres with his kit, and the Major plucked the suit from his hands and was pulling it on as the Private hit the wall.

Chef looked back at her and then his watch, "let's give it five minutes. If he's willing, Private Smith can assist the Major, and we'll see how they get on."

"Yes Sir!" said Smith

Simultaneously the Major said, "capital."

They got to work immediately. The Major called for tools as he needed them, and the Private handed them over, repeating the tools' name.

It seemed like an eternity, but in fact, it was only six minutes later the Major pulled off the hood and said "done."

They greeted the good news with a collective sigh.

"I'm guessing you don't have a bomb containment chamber?"

They shook their heads at him.

"A large pressure cooker with a couple of tea towels will do until the Squad can send someone to collect it. If you have a spare Dangerous Goods cage, we can leave it in there."

"Thank you Major," said Chef, "I'll send a private back with the cooker and tea towels, and he can show you where the cages are."

And a very little time later, the bomb was secured, the area cleaned and tidied, and it was almost as if nothing had happened.

Minty escorted the Major back to his table and had a brandy sent over to him.

She attempted to dismiss the Private, but he refused to end his shift early, so she sent him back to the function room, and arranged for a brandy sent to his quarters.

Needing a few precious moments of still, quiet time, she stood alone in the foyer, looking through the main doors and up the entry path, wrestling her composure into place.

Foiling an assassination attempt on her first day at a new post was undoubtedly more excitement than she'd imagined.

She wasn't sure she'd care to do that very often. If at all, ever again.

After a while, she became aware that the glass doors were reflecting someone standing next to her, hands clasped behind his back, and she turned to see Chef.

"Good job Lieutenant."

"Thank you Sir." She noticed a few flecks of glitter on his shoulder and reached out to brush them off.

He raised one eyebrow.

"If I may?"

He nodded, and she dusted them off, feeling a swirl of warm emotions toward her.

Then she remembered she'd taken her gloves off a hundred years ago and scrabbled in her pockets to find them and pull them on.

"There's someone who wants to meet you," he said quietly, "if you feel up to it?"

She stood to attention, and clicked her heels together, "of course Sir."

"Follow me."

He turned and led her down a side corridor to a small backstage room, opened a door and gestured her to enter.

And then closed the door behind her.

The Director General was alone in the room.

She stood to attention and saluted briskly.

"Lieutenant Hollister, I believe I owe you a great debt," he said.

"Not at all Sir, just doing my job."

"Nonetheless, I am grateful for your quick thinking."

"Thank you Sir."

"And I'd like to offer you a position in the Department of the Director General."

"Thank you Sir, but I don't see how I can help you there."

"You've demonstrated an unexpected use of your ability. It seems you may be more useful, gloves off, in a more protective capacity."

She wanted to know what the Director General hoped for, but his explicit use of the term "gloves off" suggested she didn't have permission to do that right now.

She'd have to use the usual means.

She looked up at him, studying his face and stance in a way that was hopefully not too calculating or suspicious. "Uh, thank you Sir. But I don't have training in that area."

"If it's something you want to pursue, I can fast-track your training."

She couldn't read anything either way, but rumour had it he'd ruthlessly assassinated his way into Office and you didn't do that by giving away anything a recent graduate could read.

He stood tall and straight, distinguished, and maybe a bit sexy.

Minty pictured him as she'd first seen him, surrounded, aside from his adjutant, by attractive young Officers whom he'd completely disregarded.

His immaculate uniform was spotlessly black, and his shoes were so shined they almost looked patent.

He seemed to sense her hesitation, "of course you'd have to blend in at times, sometimes you'd have to pose as a more intimate associate and wear civilian clothes. Like at events such as this."

For an instant, she could see herself on his arm wearing the long lime green, sparkly, swishy dress she'd imagined that afternoon, and wondered if he'd read her and planted the image there.

Then she remembered Chef's warm welcome, and the courtesy he showed his subordinates. And the sad smile he'd given as he opened the door to this room for her.

And there was the eager bomb-defusing Private. And all the other personnel who'd been so kind to her since she arrived just that morning.

Then there was the glitter. The glitter she'd decided would lead the way.

There was nothing glittery about the Director General, but there was glitter all around her here.

And on Chef's shoulder.

One sparkly dress couldn't compete against that.

The glitter said, stay.

She took a step back and saluted. "Thank you Sir, but I think I'm better off where I am. If that's all?"

He nodded. She spun on her heel and marched out of the room and down the corridor, away from him as fast as she could without running.

And as soon as she was a respectable distance around the corner, she bent over, retching, though she couldn't really say why.

Relief?

Disgust?

Terror?

The golden speckles in the floor seemed to reassure her, as did a warm hand on her back, "I take it you're staying then Lieutenant?" Chef asked.

"Yes Sir."

"That calls for a celebration. Why don't we quickly retire to my ready room, where there are plenty of witnesses to protect us?"

She stifled a snort, "thank you Sir."

He took her arm and half dragged, half carried her back in the kitchen's direction, "I think under the circumstances, you may, at the appropriate times, call me Josh."

"Thank you Sir, I mean Josh. And you may call me Minty."

"So Minty," he said as he pulled her over the threshold, "you've given everyone else a brandy. Would you like one too?"

"Technically, I'm still on duty Sir."

He glared at her for a moment.

"Technically, I'm still on duty, Josh."

"Under the circumstances, I think we can make an exception this time, but don't make it a habit," he said, winking.

He pulled a bottle of brandy and a couple of glasses from a drawer in his desk and poured them each a large one.

He handed one to her, and lifted his in a toast, "welcome to Cavern Caves Minty. I hope the rest of your posting proves less eventful than this."

She clinked her glass against his, "thank you Josh, I hope so too."

THE END

ABOUT THE AUTHOR

Alexandria Blaelock writes stories, some of them for *Ellery Queen's Mystery Magazine* and *Pulphouse Fiction Magazine.*

She's also written five self-help books applying business techniques to personal matters like getting dressed, cleaning house, and feeding your friends.

She lives in a forest because she enjoys birdsong, the scent of gum leaves and the sun on her face. When not telecommuting to parallel universes from her Melbourne based imagination, she watches K-dramas, talks to animals, and drinks Campari. At the same time.

Discover more at www.alexandriablaelock.com.

... or the collections

... or The Ghost and Ms Cox

Life interrupted

To say the letter was a surprise was an understatement. It arrived addressed to Miss Finlay Cox, which made the contents even more extraordinary.

Orphan Finn Cox inherits a cottage. Thinks it holds the key to her origins. Of course she takes a look. Who wouldn't?

But when she gets there, she gets more than she bargained for.

Is it friend, family or foe?